Sean "Diddy" Combs

by Z.B. Hill

Superstars of Hip-Hop

Alicia Keys

Beyoncé

Black Eyed Peas

Ciara

Dr. Dre

Drake

Eminem

50 Cent

Flo Rida

Hip Hop:
A Short History

Jay-Z

Kanye West

Lil Wayne

LL Cool J

Ludacris

Mary J. Blige

Notorious B.I.G.

Rihanna

Sean "Diddy" Combs

Snoop Dogg

T.I.

T-Pain

Timbaland

Tupac

Usher

Sean "Diddy" Combs

by Z.B. Hill

Mason Crest

Sean "Diddy" Combs

Mason Crest
370 Reed Road
Broomall, Pennsylvania 19008
www.masoncrest.com

Printed and bound in the United States of America.

First printing
9 8 7 6 5 4 3 2 1

Library of Congress Cataloging-in-Publication Data

Hill, Z. B.
  Sean "Diddy" Combs / by Z.B. Hill.
     p. cm. – (Superstars of hip hop)
  Includes index.
  ISBN 978-1-4222-2514-1 (hard cover) – ISBN 978-1-4222-2508-0 (series hardcover) – ISBN 978-1-4222-9216-7 (ebook)
  1. Diddy, 1969--Juvenile literature. 2. Rap musicians–United States–Biography–Juvenile literature. 3. Sound recording executives and producers–United States–Biography–Juvenile literature. I. Title.
  ML3930.P84H55 2012
  728.421649092–dc23
  [B]
                          2011019652

Produced by Harding House Publishing Services, Inc.
www.hardinghousepages.com
Interior Design by MK Bassett-Harvey.
Cover design by Torque Advertising & Design.

Publisher's notes:
  • All quotations in this book come from original sources and contain the spelling and grammatical inconsistencies of the original text.
  • The Web sites mentioned in this book were active at the time of publication. The publisher is not responsible for Web sites that have changed their addresses or discontinued operation since the date of publication. The publisher will review and update the Web site addresses each time the book is reprinted.

DISCLAIMER: The following story has been thoroughly researched, and to the best of our knowledge, represents a true story. While every possible effort has been made to ensure accuracy, the publisher will not assume liability for damages caused by inaccuracies in the data, and makes no warranty on the accuracy of the information contained herein. This story has not been authorized nor endorsed by Sean "Diddy" Combs.

Contents

Hip-Hop lingo

A **marathon** is a long race—about 26 miles.

A **fundraiser** raises money to help people.

If you are an **inspiration** to people, you make them want to do something and make them feel good about themselves.

A **publicity stunt** is when someone does something just to get attention.

A **charity** is a group that gives time, money, or other things to help make people's lives better.

Chapter 1

Running the Race

It was Sunday, November 2, 2003. Sean Combs and thousands of other runners jogged quietly in place. Some listened to music on headphones. Others simply took deep breaths and tried to stay calm. They waited for the gunshot that would signal the race's start. This was the New York City **Marathon**—one of the biggest races in the United States.

Sean Combs, also known as P. Diddy, was not a professional runner. He'd never run a marathon before. The New York City race was 26.2 miles long. Even for the pros, 26 miles is a long way! Diddy was not running for exercise. He was using the race as a **fundraiser**. He wanted to raise money for New York City schools. He also wanted to be an **inspiration** for others.

Diddy's kids went to private schools. As a rich man, he was able to provide a good education for his kids. But he knew that not all children were so lucky. Many depended on public schools. Some public schools didn't have a lot of money. They struggled to help their students succeed. So Diddy made a promise. If he finished the race, he and his friends would give $1 million to New York City schools.

Diddy called his race "Diddy Runs the City." He said he hoped "people become more aware of the health and educational needs that face the children of New York City." He wrote on his website, "Every child needs a high-quality education and proper health

By publicizing the "Diddy Runs the City" event, Combs was able to raise $2 million in pledges. However, this also placed pressure on him to complete the race. Failure would disappoint all the kids who could have benefited.

care in order to prepare for the 'Marathon of Life.' On Sunday, November 2, I am going to run the New York City Marathon and truly take this cause to the streets."

By 2003, Diddy had many rich and powerful friends. Actors Jennifer Lopez and Ben Affleck said they'd give $78,000. Rapper Jay-Z promised $25,000. Even the mayor of New York gave $10,000. Diddy was truly a star—and the 2003 race proved it.

Under Pressure

Diddy was excited to have his friends' support. But now he had to finish the race! The pressure was on. If he didn't finish, he would let down himself and his friends. Even worse, he'd let down the children of New York City.

When the starter's pistol fired, the runners sprang from the starting line. At first, Diddy smiled and waved at TV cameras as he ran. But the hardest part was still to come.

The Finish Line

Halfway through the race, Diddy felt like he couldn't go on. The finish line seemed so far away. Imagine running 13 miles and knowing you still have 13 more to go! But Diddy was prepared. He'd told TV reporters before the race, "It's gonna be a rough one. Probably around the thirteenth mile, I'll really need your support." His chest burned. Sweat stung his eyes. For a few minutes, it looked like Diddy would drop out of the race.

But then something amazing happened. A few children began to run next to him. They were shouting, clapping, and cheering him on! The kids reminded Diddy why he was there in the first place. They were the reason he needed to finish.

At 4 hours and 18 minutes, Diddy crossed the finish line. "The kids wouldn't let me stop," he told the *New York Daily News*. "I was running for them, and they wouldn't let me stop." Even so, some people said Diddy did the race to bring attention to himself. To them, he simply said, "Twenty-six miles is not a **publicity stunt**."

The race raised over $2 million that day. Diddy gave half the amount to New York City schools. The other half he split between

New York City mayor Michael Bloomberg, Sean Combs, Caroline Kennedy, and city schools chancellor Joel Klein pose with a large check for $2 million. Half of that money was donated to fund libraries and technology in city schools.

other worthy **charities**. These included Children's Hope Foundation and Daddy's House Social Programs.

The hip-hop star was on top of the world. He was rich, famous, and able to help others now. He'd risen higher than he ever dreamed as a little boy. "It's an honor and a blessing," he said, "to do something good for the city."

But how did he get there? And where would he go next?

Hip-Hop lingo

A **housing project** is a place where it's cheap to live. Most of the time, poor people live there.

DJ is short for disc jockey. A DJ plays music on the radio or at a party and announces the songs.

Chapter 2

Ready for Success

P. Diddy was born Sean John Combs on November 4, 1970. His family lived in Harlem, a neighborhood in New York City. Harlem was once the center of black culture and art. By the time Sean was born, though, it was a very different place.

Two of a Kind

Sean's parents were Melvin and Janice Combs. Melvin worked for the city and drove a taxi. Janice was a model. Both Melvin and Janice were very good looking. They loved style and good taste. Sean later said, "My mom . . . was like the fly girl of the neighborhood, and my pops was the fly guy . . . That's how they got together." (A fly guy or girl is someone who is really, really cool.)

Melvin and Janice worked hard to make a good life for Sean. They wanted him and his younger sister Keisha to grow up in a stable home. But no one knew how far Melvin was willing to go to make money for his family. He was selling drugs between jobs to make extra cash. He used the extra money to buy nice cars for the family. He also dressed them in fancy clothes. He got Sean a small acting part in a print ad for ice cream.

It was a small thing, but it was Sean's first taste of stardom. "As soon as that spotlight hit me, I just embraced it," he said later.

Pain Comes Early

But Melvin's double life couldn't last forever. When Sean was still a toddler, Melvin was killed. He was sitting in his car near Central Park when someone shot him. Janice wasn't ready to tell her children the full truth. So she told Sean and Keisha their father was

Sean Combs never forgot the place where he grew up. When it came time to shoot ads for his Sean John clothing line, Combs chose Harlem as the location for filming. Here he talks to neighborhood kids that have gathered around the staging area.

killed in a car accident. Sean didn't learn the whole truth until he was a teenager.

Life changed quickly after that. Janice got a full-time job to provide for her two kids. Sean went to live with his grandma, Jessie. She lived in a Harlem **housing project** called Esplanade Gardens. Diddy says Jessie's strong faith in God and her loving nature were very important to him. He learned a lot from his time with her.

Not long after, Janice found a new house for them in Mount Vernon, New York. It was in a rich neighborhood. It was a big change from Harlem. But Janice had a plan for her kids. She wanted them to stay in Harlem for a few more years. She didn't want to spoil them. She said Harlem would give them strength for later years. Later on, Diddy said that his mom turned out to be right. In Harlem, he learned to stand up to bullies and fight for himself. He learned to be a survivor.

Time for a Change

In 1982, Sean and Keisha finally joined their mother in Mount Vernon. It wasn't easy for Sean, but he accepted it. And, in time, he came to love his new home. In Mount Vernon, there was less crime, overcrowding, and drugs. Sean could focus on school and his future. He didn't need to always worry about survival.

Janice had plans for her son. She saw that he was smart. She wanted him to study hard and stay out of trouble. She told him, "Go to school and pay close attention to your teachers if you want to be a millionaire." Sean went to a private Catholic high school called Mount St. Michael Academy.

New School, New Chances

St. Michael's had its downsides. For one, no one listened to hip-hop. In Harlem, Sean had fallen in love with artists like Kool Herc,

Run-D.M.C., and KRS-One. He owned their records. He'd even gone to some of their live shows sometimes. But his white classmates listened to bands like Van Halen and Aerosmith. Even so, Sean made many friends and played on the football team. It was on the field, puffing his chest out when he was angry, that he got the nickname "Puffy."

Sean sometimes called his new home "money-earnin' Mount Vernon." That's really how he thought about it, too. He took every chance he got to make extra cash. After school and on weekends, he worked any job he could find. Sometimes his friends laughed at the silly jobs he did. But Sean didn't care. He wanted to make money. He wanted to dream big.

Around this same time, Sean became curious about his father. He still went to Harlem every few weekends. On one of these trips, he heard his grandma and her friends talking about his father. What he heard was different from what his mom had told him. He wanted to know more. So he went to the local library. There, he learned the truth. His dad's death had not been an accident.

Later, Sean said he was not angry about what he learned that day. He knew his mother had lied to protect him. But he also said that he felt better knowing the real story.

College Life

Sean did well in high school. He applied to Howard University in Washington, D.C. He was accepted. Sean was honored to go there.

He settled in and tried to focus on his studies. But he found it hard. Other interests began to draw him away from books. Music, especially, seemed to call out to him. During high school, he had danced in a few music videos. He had a longing to be in show business that never quite went away.

So he decided to start calling himself Puff Daddy. He formed a group with a classmate named Deric Angelettie. Deric was a popular **DJ**. He shared Puffy's love of hip-hop.

Together, Puffy and Deric became good at throwing parties. No one did it quite like Puffy. Everyone in Washington, D.C., wanted to join the fun. Even people from New York City heard about Puffy's parties. By day, Puffy and Deric were normal students. By night, they were party experts. One party brought 4,500 people through its doors. An entire city block had to be shut down.

It didn't take long for the news to get out. Soon, Puffy had some of the biggest names in show business knocking on his door.

Puff Daddy performs with backup dancers at the 2005 MTV Video Awards. In college, Puffy made a name for himself with his innovative dance steps, and his earliest work in music was as a backup dancer.

Hip-Hop lingo

A **label** is a company that makes music and sells CDs.

A **producer** is the person in charge of putting together songs. A producer makes the big decisions about the music.

The **media** is the group of people who create news. Media can include photographs, videos, or news articles.

To be **signed** to a label means to make a deal with a label. The artist makes records, and the label sells them.

R&B stands for "rhythm and blues." It's a kind of music that African Americans made popular in the 1940s. It has a very strong beat. Today, it's a style of music that's a lot like hip-hop.

An album goes **platinum** when it sells more than 1,000,000 copies.

A **single** is a song that is sold by itself.

Critics are people who judge artistic works and say what is good and what is bad about them.

Chapter 3

Becoming a Star

With each party, Puffy was closer to being a star. His parties allowed him to meet rich and famous people. He started to make all the right connections. Now he just needed to use those connections.

An Important Meeting

His big break came while he was still in college. Puffy had an old friend from Harlem named Heavy D. Heavy had made two albums. He was famous for his music. Heavy made hip-hop for the **label** Uptown Records. Uptown was created and run by Andre Harrell. Puffy had heard many good things about Harrell. He was a powerful African American businessman who made his money from the hip-hop scene. Puffy thought he could learn a lot from him.

So Puffy asked Heavy D to set up a meeting with Harrell. Heavy did, and Harrell was very impressed by the young man. He decided make him an intern at Uptown. Interns do all the work of a regular employee. Usually, they don't get paid. Instead, they work for experience. This was a perfect setup for Puffy. Even though he didn't get cash, he learned the skills he would use later in life to become a millionaire.

Puffy worked harder than anyone at Uptown. If other people worked 8 hours, Puffy worked 10 or 12. During meetings, he took notes and paid attention. He knew this was the life he wanted.

In 1991, his hard work paid off. Harrell offered Puffy a full-time job. He accepted and dropped out of college. His decision upset his mother. But he felt it was the right thing to do.

The High Life

The perks of the new job came quickly to Puffy. Harrell moved him into a beautiful mansion in New Jersey. He gave Puffy nice cars to drive and a swimming pool. A limo picked Puffy up from work and drove him to the finest restaurants. Most days ended at a club for a night of partying. It was a big change from his old life.

It wasn't all play, though. Puffy had to earn everything. His job was to bring new artists to Uptown Records. If the people Puffy brought in didn't sell records, Puffy had failed. It was a lot of pressure for a young man. But he was ready for anything.

At first, Puffy tried to keep it simple. He didn't try to bring lots of attention to himself. But then he had another idea. At Howard University, having a flashy image helped him succeed. In the music business, the same thing seemed to work. Many music **producers** brought lots of **media** attention to themselves. So Puffy decided to do the same. It was a risk, but it worked. Puffy told *Paper* magazine, "I've never let anyone down who was willing to take a chance on me."

Puffy began to dress the part of a famous producer. He wore expensive clothes and jewelry. Not long after, he got his first big chance. Uptown Records **signed** a group called Jodeci. The boys in the group were still very young. They came from a small town. They knew very little about show business. They really needed Puffy's help.

He didn't let them down. Jodeci wanted to be like another male **R&B** group called Boyz II Men. But there were plenty of those

Through his association with Andre Harrell and Uptown Records, Puff Daddy was ushered into the world of luxurious living. In this 2005 photo, Harrell (at left) and Combs are pictured here attending a fashion show in New York City.

groups already. Puffy took them in a different direction. Most male groups tried to dress like very rich people. Puffy told Jodeci to look like normal guys. He got his girlfriend, Misa Hylton, to help him dress the group.

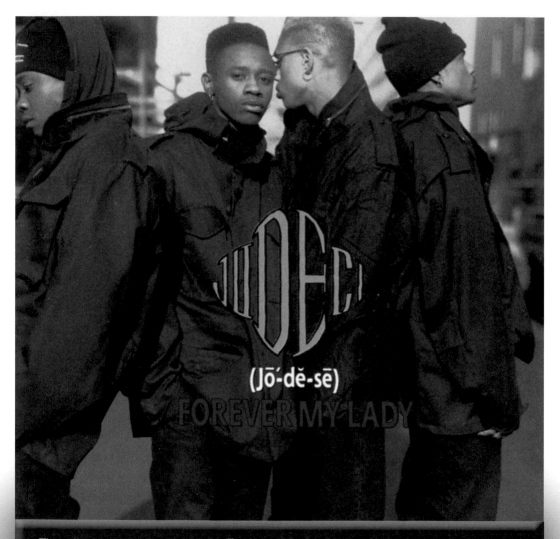

The album cover for Jodeci's *Forever My Lady* shows the group in their urban street look. Along with the trend-setting fashion sense that Puffy suggested, the boys had a musical sound that was unique.

This is where Puffy really began to shine. He dressed Jodeci in colored baseball caps, sweatshirts, and baggy jeans. In other words, he dressed them nicely—but they still looked like normal guys. Teenagers really loved their look. This was an image they could relate to.

But Puffy didn't stop there. He gave them musical help, too. Puffy was sure that hip-hop had a place in R&B. Until the early 1990s, the two types of music were rarely combined. Puffy added a hip-hop edge to Jodeci's songs that really worked. Their 1991 album, *Forever My Lady*, went **platinum**—twice!

A Girl Named Mary

Puffy was happy with Jodeci's success. But he knew a producer needed more than one success. He needed another hit artist. He needed someone to take him to even greater heights.

That someone's name was Mary J. Blige. As a young girl, she sang in the church choir. She had talent, and her friends told her to make a recording of her singing. She did, and the tape found its way to Jeff Redd. He also worked for Uptown. He liked what he heard. Puffy was chosen to produce her first album. Little did he know, big things were about to happen.

Almost right away, the producer and his star ran into problems. Puffy wanted Mary to have a certain image. He wanted her to dress and act as if she were already famous. Mary didn't want to show off her money in front of her poor family and friends. But eventually, she agreed to try it. The combo of living a wealthy life in a poor neighborhood became known as "ghetto fabulous." Yet again, Puffy's eye for image had started another hit trend.

Mary and Puffy's problems quickly went away. Their first album was called *What's the 411?* It came out in 1992 and was a huge hit. It sold 2 million copies and had a number-one **single** called

Puff Daddy poses with one of his stars, Mary J. Blige, at the second annual Hip-Hop Summit Action Awards dinner in 2004. Mary was just a girl from the projects until her demo tape made its way to Uptown and Puffy.

"Real Love." **Critics** loved the album, and they loved Mary. They compared her to great singers such as Billie Holiday and Aretha Franklin!

Once again, Puffy added a hip-hop touch. And once again, people liked it. Puffy was creating a unique style.

Puffy's work as a producer made Mary J. Blige a phenomenon. Her rise to fame was sometimes even more than she could handle. She was expected to perform in front of large crowds, including the 2003 NFL Kickoff Concert shown here.

A Good Thing Goes Bad

Puffy's good luck was about to run out, though. Puffy put together a charity concert. It would be a fundraiser for a group called AIDS Education Outreach. He called it the "Heavy D and Puff Daddy First Annual Celebrity Basketball Game." It was supposed to happen just after Christmas Day in 1991. Puffy invited Jodeci, Boyz II Men, and A Tribe Called Quest. The concert would take place at a college gymnasium.

Sean "Puffy" Combs talks to reporters in 1998 after testifying at a lawsuit over the deaths at a 1991 City College concert. The courts decided that in addition to Puffy, many other parties were to blame for the accidental deaths.

The concert was a big deal. Thousands of people lined up to see the amazing show. Sadly, too many people came to see the musicians. Almost 5,000 people tried to fit into a gym that could only hold 2,700. The crowd got too excited before the concert. People began to push and shove toward the doors. Nine people were crushed and died. A fun night of music turned into a terrible and sad day.

Many people blamed Puffy for the deaths. Even though lots of people planned the concert, Puffy took the most blame. He was the most famous, so people pointed their fingers at him.

It turned out that lots of things had gone wrong. It wasn't Puffy's fault alone. The police didn't properly control the crowd. The college didn't have enough security there. And the medical services people were slow to respond. Everyone had made mistakes.

But Puffy kept taking heat for the accident. Some people even said the charity was a fake. No one in the AIDS service community had heard of the "AIDS Education Outreach Program." In fact, there was no record of any charity under that name. It looked bad for Puffy.

He felt miserable. For the first time, he faced a big failure. Old friends and businesspeople wouldn't return his calls. Uptown Records asked him to stay away from the office for a while. The only people who stood by him were his mother, his girlfriend Misa, and his lawyers. Puffy later said that only his faith in God got him through that awful time.

Hip-Hop lingo

A **demo** is a rough, early version of a CD before the real thing comes out.

Lyrics are the words in a song.

A **feud** is a fight between two people or groups that goes on for a long time.

Something that is **classic** is likely to be popular for a long time.

Chapter 4

Trouble at the Top

After the accident, Puffy was very sad. He spent several months at home. But he soon bounced back. Life goes on, and Puffy had big plans.

Big Changes

In 1993, Puffy got his next big break. He began working with a rapper named Christopher Wallace, also known as Notorious B.I.G. (or Biggie Smalls.) Biggie had a talent for rapping. He made a short **demo**, and the tape found its way to Puffy. Right away, the producer heard something special.

"When I first met Biggie, he was real quiet and shy," Puffy told *MTV News*. Biggie was also six foot three inches tall and weighed over 300 pounds. No one could miss him. More important, he had talent. His **lyrics** were smart. They could sell records.

Slowly, Puffy got Biggie ready for stardom. He let him rap on some of Mary J. Blige's songs. He even put one of Biggie's songs on a movie soundtrack.

Puffy's personal life was good, too. In 1993, his girlfriend Misa gave birth to a baby boy named Justin. Everything was good in Puffy's world. But another failure was just around the corner.

Parting from Uptown

In 1993, Andre Harrell fired Puffy from Uptown Records. Uptown felt Puffy was too full of himself and that he didn't listen to his superiors.

It was a huge loss for Puffy. He cried for days. He later said he felt like he was going through a divorce. After all, Uptown had been Puffy's life. He'd poured his hopes and dreams into it.

But Puffy wasn't out of the game that easily. Other music label owners saw Puffy's talent. They offered him high-paying jobs. Puffy refused. He had even bigger plans for himself. He wanted to start his own label.

He got his chance when Clive Davis called. Davis owned Arista Records. He had the money and the power to help Puffy succeed. He would back Puffy's new label for a share of the profits. Puffy accepted, and the deal was sealed. Davis had a lot of confidence in his new business partner. He told *Billboard*, "Puffy has a feel for the street and combines it with an unusual grasp of what can best bring it to the marketplace."

Some people didn't think Puffy could make it alone. Puffy wasn't bothered by them, though. "People are going to say what they will," he told *Newsweek*, "particularly when you're young, black, and successful."

On His Own

Puffy called his new label Bad Boy Entertainment. He decided to make his mom the owner. She had stood by him through tough times. He wanted to thank her. It was a new start for Puffy. To

Music industry legend Clive Davis, the founder of Arista Records, is pictured with Whitney Houston, whom he signed to a recording contract when she was a teenager. Davis had an eye for talent, and supported Puffy's dream of forming his own rap label.

remind himself to stay focused, he hung a sign in his office. It said, "Life Is Not A Game."

Money poured in. Puffy signed star after star to his new label. He got new artists like rapper Craig Mack and singer Faith Evans. He also brought Biggie along with him. This turned out to be one of his best moves. Biggie's first album, *Ready to Die*, became a major hit. It sold more than 4 million copies and won many awards.

To this day, many people say *Ready to Die* is one of the great hip-hop albums.

Mary J. Blige stayed at Uptown Records. But Puffy took over as her manager. This meant he continued to produce her songs and collect money on her success. Her next album, *My Life*, was a big hit. Meanwhile, Puffy kept busy signing artists like 112 and Total. He produced songs for Lil' Kim, TLC, Mariah Carey, and Boyz II Men. Nothing seemed to slow him down.

Things Get Violent

On the West Coast, a type of hip-hop called "gangsta rap" became popular. It used lyrics about the streets and talked about Los Angeles gang life. One of the most successful labels on the West Coast was Death Row Records.

Puffy had no reason to dislike Death Row Records. His number-one artist was Biggie. Death Row's number-one artist was Tupac Shakur. Everyone was friendly—for a time. But then both sides came to dislike each other. The fight grew into a **feud**. Through 1995 and 1996, they traded insults. In 1996, Tupac was shot and killed. Puffy and Biggie said they had nothing to do with it. In fact, no evidence has ever linked them to the murder. It could have been anyone. Tupac had many enemies besides Bad Boy.

But things got worse. In 1997, Biggie was shot and killed. He and Puffy were at a party together in L.A. They got into two cars and left. When Biggie's car stopped at a red light, another car pulled up beside his. Someone opened fire and Biggie was shot to death. He was only 24 years old.

Puffy was there when it happened. "I jumped out of my car and ran over to his," he later told *The New York Daily News*. "I was saying the Lord's Prayer and Hail Marys. I was begging God to help him out. I was touching him and talking to him in his ear." But nothing he did could save the young man. Biggie died at the Los Angeles Hospital.

Remembering a Friend

Biggie's death was a huge loss for Puffy. He lost a client and a best friend. He promised to take care of Biggie's family. He also called for an end to the violence between East and West Coasts.

Death Row recording artists Tupac Shakur (left) and Snoop Doggy Dogg (center) pose with the founder of Death Row Records, Marion "Suge" Knight. Los Angeles-based Death Row helped popularize the "gangsta rap" sound of the West Coast.

Two weeks after his death, Biggie's second album came out. It was called *Life After Death*. It sold 10 million copies and became a hip-hop **classic**. Critics loved it, too. Biggie didn't live long enough

Rapper Notorious B.I.G. (also known as Biggie Smalls) poses at the 1995 *Billboard* Music Awards. Biggie quickly became Puffy's good friend and Bad Boy's biggest star. The Brooklyn rapper's debut, *Ready to Die*, was hugely successful.

to enjoy its success. But it became proof of the great work Biggie and Puffy did together.

Puffy decided to do a song to honor his friend. He teamed up with Biggie's wife, singer Faith Evans. Together they made a song called "I'll Be Missing You." The song was a smash hit. Many people related to the sadness of losing a loved one. But some people said Puffy made the song just for money. Puffy proved them wrong, though. He gave all money made from the song to Biggie's family.

Faith Evans and Sean Combs announce the release of their tribute to Biggie Smalls, "I'll Be Missing You." Some critics accused Bad Boy of trying to profit from Biggie's death, but proceeds from the hit went into a fund for Biggie's kids.

Making His Own Music

In 1997, Puff Daddy made his first solo album. He called it *No Way Out*. It became an instant hit. Puffy explained the title to *Spin*: "At times, I feel like I'm trapped inside a movie starring me, but I'm not the director, and I don't know what the scene is, nothing."

Puff Daddy holds up his Grammy won in 1998 for Best Rap Album for his debut release, *No Way Out.* He also won a Grammy that year for Best Rap Performance by a Duo for "I'll Be Missing You" with Faith Evans.

The record was full of Bad Boy stars. Together, they helped make *No Way Out* a hit. Many critics did not like the album. But that hardly bothered Puffy. He had millions of fans who bought the record. That was enough for him.

Other successes followed. In 1997, Puffy produced one of the best albums of the 1990s. He helped make Mariah Carey's *Butterfly*. It sold 235,000 copies in its first week! Puffy got credit for adding a hip-hop edge to Carey's music.

Also, Puffy continued to turn unknown artists into stars. He helped out rapper Ma$e in 1996. Not a year later, Ma$e was one of the biggest names in hip-hop. Clearly, Puffy was at the top of his game. He seemed unable to fail.

Personal Life

Puffy broke up with his girlfriend Misa Hylton. Soon after, he had and his new girlfriend, Kim Porter, had a baby. The couple named their son Christian.

Things were up and down for Puffy. He was still working out his personal life. But one thing was certain: he was one of hip-hop's biggest stars.

Hip-Hop lingo

A **starring role** is one of the most important parts in the movie or television show.

Chapter 5

A Bright Future

Bad Boy was now Puffy's main interest. He was working hard at bringing in new talent. It was a new page in the story of Puffy's life. So he decided he needed a new name, too. "No more Puffy Daddy," he told MTV. "It is going to be changed to straight P. Diddy. You could call me P., or Diddy, or P. Diddy."

Diddy Takes on the World

With a new name came new chances for even bigger fame. Diddy acted in a movie called *Monster's Ball*. It won many awards. People gave Diddy respect for taking part in such a great movie. In 2004, he had a **starring role** in *A Raisin in the Sun* on Broadway.

He didn't stop there. In 1998, Diddy created his own clothing line. He called it Sean John. Since it started, Sean John has sold millions of dollars of clothing. People love Diddy's fashion sense. His unique style has won him awards, too. In 2004, he won an award for Best Menswear.

He's also made moves in the food business. In 1997, he started his own restaurant, called Justin's. It serves Southern food and food from the Caribbean Islands. Diddy says he's serious about making great food. "I'm not just a talker. I open up a restaurant and I keep it open," he said.

Helping Others

Diddy loves to help people who need it. That's why he started Daddy's House. It's a charity for kids and teens. It helps poor kids get a good education. It teaches teens about how to save money. And it even helps high school seniors find the right college.

He also started Daddy's House International Travel. It helps inner-city kids fly around the world. He pays for them to see other

Seagrams CEO Edgar Bronfman, Jr. and Sean Combs work on a house as part of a Habitat for Humanity project in September 2005. The organization was constructing new homes to replace houses in the South that had been destroyed by Hurricane Katrina.

On MTV's Total Request Live in 2004, Combs promotes a get-out-the-vote campaign for the presidential election. With the slogan "Vote or Die," he hoped to make voting trendy and popular among young people who might not otherwise turn out at the polls.

cultures. They study other places and bring what they learn back to the United States.

Vote or Die

Many young people don't vote. Before the 2004 elections, Diddy worked to fix this problem. He came up with the phrase "vote or die." He made t-shirts and hats and even went on TV to get out his message. He wanted young people to know that voting is important. If no one votes, he said, our country is not in our control.

Staying Successful

Sean Combs seems to have success in everything he does. Today, he's working hard to keep it that way!

In 2010, Diddy released a new album with his group Dirty Money. The album was called *Last Train to Paris*. Diddy's new album was a success. The album showed that Diddy could still make music that people loved.

Diddy is busy with much more than music these days, though! He told CNN he might even open a business school in New York City. He's also announced plans for a business school and a television network called Revolt. Revolt will be focused on music, Diddy says.

In 2012, Combs won his first Academy Award for the film *Undefeated*. Combs was executive producer on the high school football documentary. Music isn't the only business that Diddy knows. And there doesn't seem to be anything that he can't succeed in. Fans are excited to see what's next from the mogul and music superstar!

Producer, rapper, actor, fashion designer, restaurant owner, and much more—Sean Combs has done it all. And yet he's stayed hungry for what the future holds. He told *Vox* magazine: "I've still got a long way to go to make the type of impact I want to make."

1970   Sean Combs is born on November 4 in New York City.

1972   Sean's father, Melvin Combs, is shot to death on January 26.

1982   Janice Combs moves her children to Mount Vernon, New York.

1987   Sean Combs graduates from Mount St. Michael Academy and begins attending Howard University.

1988   Meets Uptown Records founder Andre Harrell.

1991   Andre Harrell names Puffy head of Artists & Repertoire at Uptown. Puffy produces his first album for the group Jodeci, the hugely successful *Forever My Lady*. Nine people die of asphyxiation on December 27 at a basketball event organized by Puffy.

1992   Produces Mary J. Blige's album *What's the 411?*, which becomes an overnight sensation after it is released on July 28.

1993   Begins working with Biggie Smalls (The Notorious B.I.G.); after being fired from Uptown Records, starts Bad Boy Entertainment and signs a distribution agreement with Clive Davis of Arista Records.

1994   First child, a boy named Justin, is born to Misa Hylton; Bad Boy releases the Notorious B.I.G.'s first album, *Ready to Die*, on September 13; rapper Tupac Shakur is shot in a New York recording studio on November 30, but survives.

1995   The bitter East Coast–West Coast rap feud develops between Bad Boy Entertainment and Death Row Records.

1996   Tupac is shot and killed in Las Vegas during September.

1997   In March, Biggie Smalls is shot and killed in Los Angeles; *No Way Out*, Puff Daddy's first album as a performer, is released on July 22; Puffy performs his hit "I'll Be Missing You," a tribute to Biggie Smalls, with Faith Evans and Sting at MTV's *Video Music Awards.*

1998   Second child, a boy named Christian, is born to Kim Porter on March 30; Puffy debuts his clothing line, Sean John.

1999   On August 24, Puff Daddy's second album, *Forever*, is released; he is arrested after a shooting at a New York nightclub on December 27.

2001   On March 16, Puffy is acquitted of weapons charges in the nightclub shooting; changes name to P. Diddy; receives critical acclaim for his performance in the film *Monster's Ball.*

2002   Stars in *Making the Band 2* on MTV.

2003   Successfully completes the New York City Marathon on November 2, raising $2 million for charity.

2004   Makes his Broadway debut in *A Raisin in the Sun* on April 26.

2006   Introduces his designer fragrance, *Unforgivable*, in January; he is also accused and found guilty of using the real animal fur of raccoon dogs after advertising his line as using faux fur.

2007   Sean Combs goes on his *American Gangster* tour.

2008   Diddy buys the *Enyce* clothing line from Liz Claiborne for $20 million.

2010   Diddy releases *Last Train to Paris* with Dirty Money.

In Books

Baker, Soren. *The History of Rap and Hip Hop*. San Diego, Calif.: Lucent, 2006.

Comissiong, Solomon W. F. *How Jamal Discovered Hip-Hop Culture*. New York: Xlibris, 2008.

Cornish, Melanie. *The History of Hip Hop*. New York: Crabtree, 2009.

Czekaj, Jef. *Hip and Hop, Don't Stop!* New York: Hyperion, 2010.

Haskins, Jim. *One Nation Under a Groove: Rap Music and Its Roots*. New York: Jump at the Sun, 2000.

Hatch, Thomas. *A History of Hip-Hop: The Roots of Rap*. Portsmouth, N.H.: Red Bricklearning, 2005.

Websites

Bad Boy
www.badboyonline.com

Diddy, Dirty Money
www.diddydirtymoney.com/splash

MTV: Sean Combs
www.mtv.com/music/artist/puff_daddy/artist.jhtml

Sean Combs on the New York Daily News
www.nydailynews.com/topics/Sean+Combs

Sean John Clothing
www.seanjohn.com

Discography
Albums

1997	No Way Out
1999	Forever
2001	The Saga Continues
2002	We Invented the Remix
2006	Press Play
2010	Last Train to Paris

Index

About the Author

Z.B. Hill is a an author and publicist living in Binghamton, New York. He has a special interest in adolescent education and how music can be used in the classroom.

Picture Credits

A. Turner/J Records/NMI: p. 31
Gary Hershorn/Reuters: p. 36
KRT/Nicolas Khayat: p. 8
KRT/Olivier Douliery: p. 25, 28
Lawrence Agron/Dreamstime: p. 1
Mitch Gerber/Star Max: p. 21
NMI/Death Row Records: p. 33
NMI/Michelle Feng: p. 22
Paul Cunningham/Ace Pictures: p. 14
Richard B. Levine/PS: p. 10
Ronald Asadorian/Splash News: p. 12
UPI/Ezio Petersen: p. 26, 35
UPI/Laura Cavanaugh: p. 38
UPI/Monika Graff: p. 6
Zuma Press/Aviv Small: p. 24
Zuma Press/Jane Caine: p. 34
Zuma Press/Nancy Kaszerman: p. 18, 40, 41
Zuma Press/NMI: p. 17